THE FAIRIES

Photographic Evidence of the Existence of Another World

BY SUZA SCALORA

JOANNA COTLER BOOKS
An Imprint of HarperCollinsPublishers

An archeologist by trade, I spend a lot of my time poring over ancient texts and obscure manuscripts in search of missing pieces to the puzzle of our history. Knowing my passion for such things, my colleagues in New York, and sometimes my students, pass along anything they think might interest me. So I wasn't surprised when I answered my door one day and found a manila envelope at my feet. A young woman in a vivid yellow dress—a student, I thought—waved back to me as she ran down the corridor. She was gone before I could thank her.

The envelope read: "When an old friend of ours passed on without warning, he left this unfinished. We hope it is something that will interest you." It was unsigned. I opened the envelope and pulled out a lovely, leather-bound manuscript. It looked like it was from the late nineteenth century, but it was in perfect condition. I took it over to my desk for a closer look. It was titled *Field Guide to Fairies*, and according to the introduction, it contained, among other things, categories of fairies and their specific characteristics, reports on sightings, peak sighting seasons, and an ancient Gaelic compendium of fairies and other elementals.

I was surprised to see this scholarly treatment of fairies, and skeptical, since as an archeologist I am driven by hard facts. Nevertheless, as I thumbed through the pages, my curiosity got the better of me. The author was a British anthropologist from the late nineteenth century, and despite the odd topic, the writing was logical and scientific. I came upon a chapter on how to attract fairies, where he speculated (based on details he had drawn from reports on sightings) that fairies could be lured into revealing themselves if the right combination of elements to which they were attracted were brought together. This is, of course, how humans have always lured creatures in the natural world, from catching fish by

baiting hooks, to attracting butterflies with specific flowers. The only thing that seemed unusual was that he was talking about fairies.

What followed was a comprehensive list of fairies throughout the world, along with elements associated with them. For instance, one fairy species native to the northeastern United States, the Yellow-Green Woodland Fairy, is said to have a great affinity for lilac bushes, honey, butterflies, fresh herbs, and the noonday sun. Others are attracted to riverbed rocks, spruce trees, twilight, rainfall, quartz, fireflies, loud noise, precious gems—to name just a few. He went on to write that the fairies of Hampstead Heath, where he lived, were said to be attracted to lavender and rosemary. It was there that he had decided to put his theories to the test. Captivated, I turned the page.

It was blank! All that followed were empty pages. I couldn't believe it. I flipped through it again, and this time a loose photo fluttered out and landed on my lap. It was of a small, winged, womanlike creature in the woods, leaning against a silver birch tree. She was staring directly into the camera. The photo, taken with a pinhole camera[1] was old and cracked, but the haunting creature shone through like a beacon. There was a look in her eyes, a hyperintensity that convinced me she came from beyond the human plane. My common sense told me that there was no such thing as a fairy, but in my heart I knew she was real.

I lifted the photo into the sunlight to get a better look. Immediately, it began to fade, and before I could do anything, the image was gone entirely. I stared at the blank photo in disbelief. I tilted it to see if some reflection of the scene remained, but there was nothing there. My heart sank as I realized that I had probably just destroyed the only evidence of fairies in the whole world.

---

1. *Pinhole camera: The pinhole camera was the first camera invented. It is a box with light-sensitive paper placed at one end and a pinhole for a lens at the other. Light from the subject matter enters through the pinhole and falls, upside down, on the light-sensitive paper inside the camera to create an image.*

The following morning, I went to the library and studied every book I could find on fairies. Aside from fairy tales and folklore, all I came across were occasional descriptions and reports on sightings, some of which were also included in the manuscript I had. Nowhere was there any mention of lures or methods of attracting fairies.

Finally, I turned away from the books and closed my eyes. I recalled what I could of the photograph and that strange creature. What was she? Where did she come from? As I clung to her image, it slowly slipped from my grasp and faded away. Then out of nowhere another image flashed through my mind, the old leather case in the corner of my closet that held my camera.

Later that day, I went to Bear Mountain, New York, in search of the Yellow-Green Woodland Fairy, who is most often seen in the early summer. I spent several hours setting up my ingredients in various ways in front of the lilac bushes. I met with no success. The following day, I also returned home empty-handed. On the third day, the thrill was starting to fade, and I began to feel a little silly hunting for fairies in New York. By noon I had almost given up. I looked at my "lure"—a pile of fresh peppermint, rosemary, and other herbs, and a jar of honey. Halfheartedly, I arranged the herbs and some lilacs in the honey jar and placed it in the sun. Two little white butterflies, attracted by the honey, settled on the rim of the jar. There was something pleasing about the arrangement—like a painting.

Suddenly there she was, leaning down to pluck a lilac petal, a small green creature with delicate yellow wings that sparkled in the sun. She looked up at me as I fumbled for my camera. I struggled to open the case and dropped it. And when I turned back to the fairy, she was gone.

I had seen a fairy! That moment changed everything for me. My heart was pounding, and I lay down in the grass, breathing heavily. I was so overwhelmed that I didn't even care that I'd dropped the camera. The butterflies flew away from the lure and fluttered past me. They rose toward the trees, spiraling around each other, and disappeared among the branches of a sycamore. Above, vast fields of cirrus clouds rippled in the stratosphere and the wake of a jet cut a clear white line across the southern sky. My mind grew silent. I took a deep breath, sat up, and watched the jet vanish in the distance.

That night I packed my bags, took the manuscript and my camera, and headed for the airport, where I set out across the world to catalog and photograph every fairy I could find. I zigzagged around the globe, jumping back and forth between continents, as I rushed to catch the peak sighting seasons of the various fairies. Some fairies I found on the very first day, others took me weeks to find, and some I never found at all. Some I saw in the distance, and no matter what I did I couldn't get close enough for a photograph. But every encounter left me filled with wonder and exhilarated beyond belief. The reality of what I saw far surpassed what I ever could have imagined possible.

—S.S.

PLATE I

EUGENIE

COMMON NAME: Eugenie, the Emerald Forest Fairy

OTHER NAME: Elvine Wood Nymph

SIGHTING DATE: July 12, 1998, 2:10 p.m.

SIGHTING LOCATION: Uxmal, Yucatan Peninsula, Mexico

PEAK SIGHTING SEASON: Early June and early July; midday, with sun directly overhead[2]

HISTORY: Little is known of Eugenie, except that she is a guardian of trees and that she changes color and markings to blend with her surroundings. She is also known as a mischief maker.

LURE: Pencils

NOTES: I found a clearing in the forest, where I set up my tripod and placed my journal on a tree stump to make notes. I walked off into the woods to take some photos, and when I returned, my pencil was gone. So I pulled out another pencil and wrote for a minute. When I turned my back to get out my camera, I heard a noise. I whirled around. My pencil had vanished again! My heart began to pound. I pulled out another pencil and purposely turned around, pretending to retrieve something from my bag. Out of the corner of my eye, I saw Eugenie speed by, snatch up the pencil, and hide behind a tree. I walked toward the tree, and she came out from behind it. She laughed at me and sprinted away. When I returned to the clearing, my notebook was gone.

2. *Eugenie uses the shadows as camouflage and so is most easily sighted when the sun is directly overhead and she has nowhere to hide.*

PLATE II

T W Y L A

COMMON NAME: Twyla, the Twilight-Blue Fairy

OTHER NAMES: Fairy of the Cloud Forest, Fading Light Fairy

SIGHTING DATE: August 17, 1998, 7:31 p.m.

SIGHTING LOCATION: Monteverde Cloud Forest, Costa Rica

PEAK SIGHTING SEASON: Height of wet season; river flooding

HISTORY: All reported sightings of Twyla have taken place along a stream that runs through the cloud forest. She appears briefly after sunset along the banks of the stream and watches it flow. According to a local fable, she is observing the passage of time, and she appears at twilight to mark the end of the day. A few hundred years ago sightings were frequent, but as people have moved into the area, Twyla has retreated. The last reported sighting was in 1923.

LURE: Instant camera

NOTES: I really had no idea of how to lure Twyla, and the task was that much more difficult because she avoids people. I chose the camera because photos are records of a moment in time, and I hoped that this would appeal to her sensibilities. As it turned out, my instincts were right. She appeared at dusk and snatched it up, and for a minute we stood opposite each other, the stream flowing between us, and I allowed her to capture me on film. She then abandoned the camera and turned her attention to the stream. I photographed her before she leapt up and vanished into the dense, dark jungle, taking the instant photos with her.

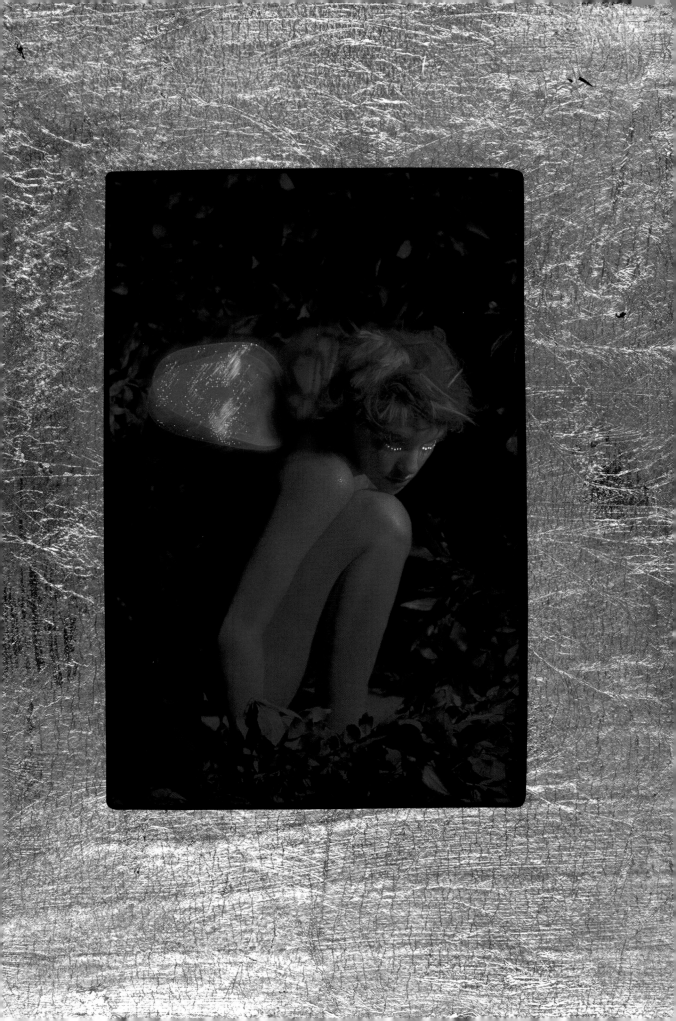

PLATE III

MALI

COMMON NAME: Mali, the Magenta Bird Fairy
OTHER NAMES: Fairy of the Dawn, Eastern Sky Fairy
SIGHTING DATE: September 23, 1998, 5:58 a.m.
SIGHTING LOCATION: Caroni Swamp, Trinidad, West Indies
PEAK SIGHTING SEASON: Tropical storm season
HISTORY: Mali comes from the class of air fairy that governs the beginning of the day, and she has been sighted throughout the Caribbean. Island natives told me that Mali is associated with birdsong. She is most frequently seen on a tiny island in Trinidad's Caroni Swamp that is also the nesting place of the scarlet ibis.
LURE: Colorful helium balloons released into the air
NOTES: I took a boat to the island at dusk, as thousands of scarlet ibises descended on it. I tied the balloons to a branch and fell asleep. I awakened before dawn to the beating of wings as the ibises lifted into the indigo sky. I released the balloons. Mali appeared through the brush, and I managed to snap a photo before she flew up and retrieved them. She tied them back on the branch, then followed the ibises in their flight down the coast.

PLATE IV

VIVIAN

COMMON NAME: Vivian, the Black Swan Fairy
OTHER NAMES: Black River Witch; Vivian the Ruthless
SIGHTING DATE: November 7, 1998, 11:59 p.m.
SIGHTING LOCATION: Porto Alegre, Brazil
PEAK SIGHTING SEASON: Wisteria in bloom
HISTORY: Some experts suggest that Vivian may not be a fairy, but some kind of ancient witch that was once human. According to Brazilian folklore, Vivian is intolerant of humans and will cast spells on those who cross her path, causing them to take the form of animals. A forest at the edge of the river is carefully avoided because of a legend that Vivian favors the area in late spring.
LURE: Trespass of her domain
NOTES: It had been six weeks since my last sighting, and I was anxious to find another fairy. I followed a path through the forest toward the river. It was an eerie, dark forest with an unsettlingly large animal population. I reached the shore and immediately saw Vivian racing across the lake toward me. In a flash she was at the water's edge. She flew up above me and shrieked. I went numb. She let out a long wail that pierced my head. I tumbled to the ground as a strange energy surged through my body, weakening me. At that moment, a yellow form[3] appeared out of nowhere, swiped at Vivian's wing, and flew out across the river. Vivian bellowed and chased after it. Three huge black feathers[4] drifted down toward me, and as they fell into my hand I felt suddenly whole again.

3. *PLATE V, Unknown Fairy, following page.*
4. *To this day, I keep those feathers next to my body at all times. The only time I was apart from them for a few hours, my vision lost color and my hearing grew so sharp that I could hear insects walking on the window.*

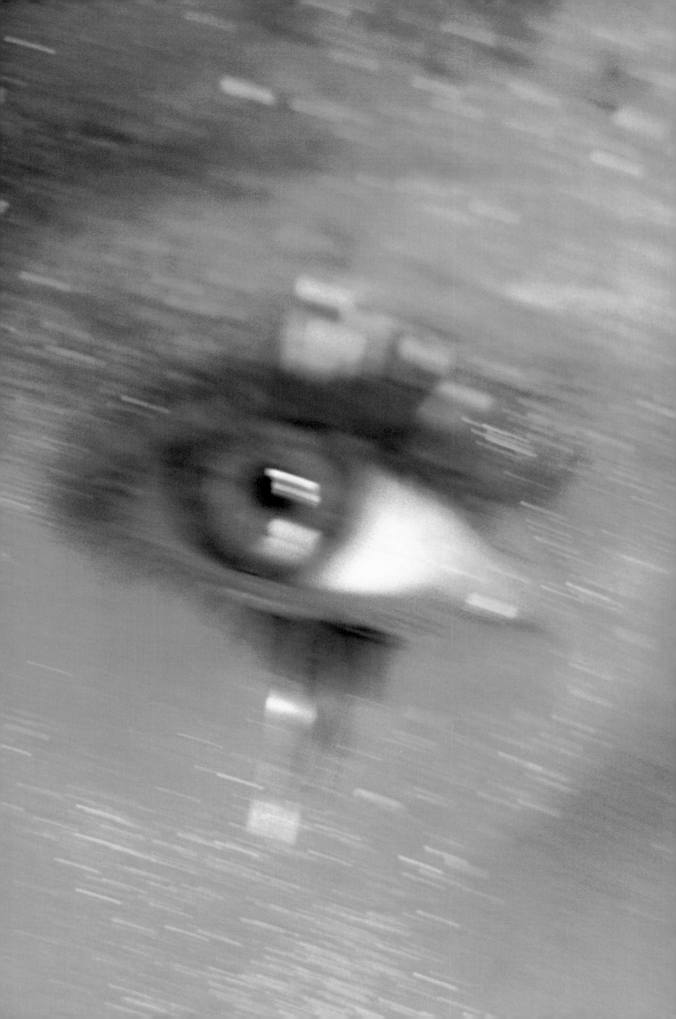

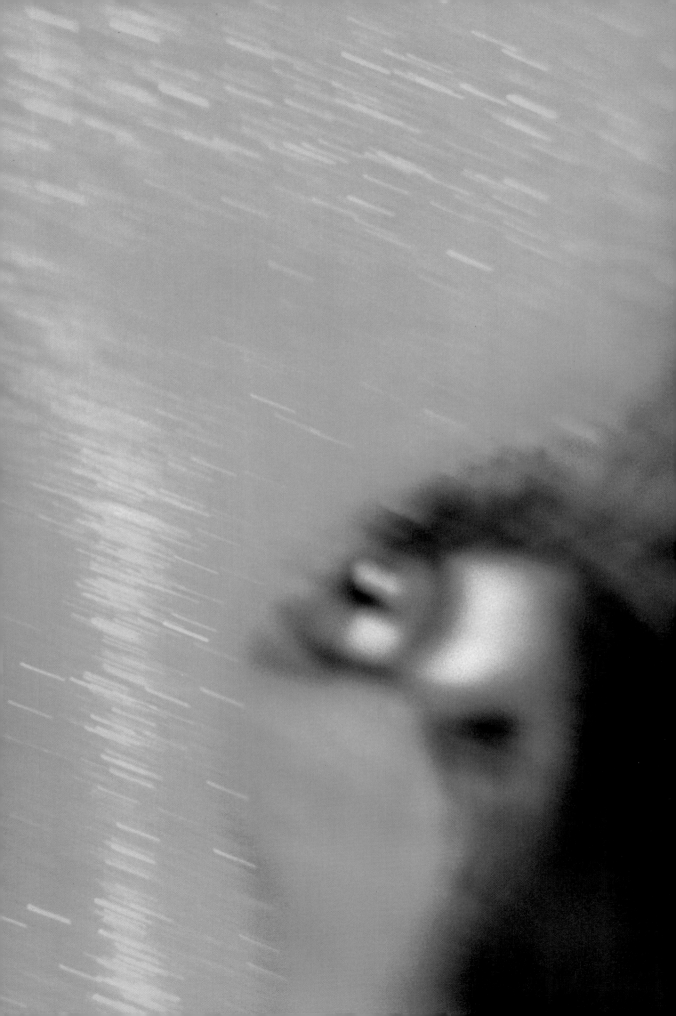

PLATE VI

THERA

COMMON NAME: Thera, the Blue Ice Fairy
OTHER NAME: Fairy of Solitude
SIGHTING DATE: December 21, 1998, dawn
SIGHTING LOCATION: Locked in a glacier in the Icelandic highlands
PEAK SIGHTING SEASON: Winter solstice
HISTORY: Thera, also known as the Keeper of Memory, is said to reside in a temple in Iceland's oldest glacier. Local lore records that among the endless reflections within this kaleidoscopic temple of ice are the records of every moment of this planet's history. Locked in an icy tableau, Thera waits for the day when the sun will release her.
LURE: Salt thrown across the face of the glacier
NOTES: Knowing she craved sunshine, I chose the shortest day of the year, and the dawn of its half hour of daylight. In the predawn light I hiked through jagged lava fields toward the colossal glacier. I arrived at the southernmost section of the glacier wall just in time, and as the sun began to rise I threw the salt. And there she was, staring out at me through the blue ice. She was motionless, but as the minutes passed and the light grew brighter, she seemed slowly to come alive. Her gaze shifted toward me. Then I felt a coolness; the sun had slipped away, the ice was silent, and Thera was gone.

PLATE VII

ARIEL

COMMON NAME: Ariel, the Crimson Sky Fairy
OTHER NAME: Evening Dream Fairy
SIGHTING DATE: January 21, 1999, 9:35 p.m.
SIGHTING LOCATION: Ravenshoe, Queensland, Australia
PEAK SIGHTING SEASON: Trade winds, summer
HISTORY: Ariel comes from a large class of air fairies that inhabit different parts of the sky and land. She lives in the rising air currents above valleys and descends into the trees after sunset.
LURE: Fireflies released into the wind
NOTES: I climbed a tree and released the fireflies. I was afraid that they'd all fly away in different directions, but instead they hovered around the branches of a tree. As my eyes adjusted, I saw Ariel in the midst of them, just a few feet away. She looked at me with the intense curiosity of a small child, and she studied the leaves, the fireflies, and the night sky with the same look of wonder. At that moment, I also found myself mesmerized by the leaves and the sky. It was as though the world was made new by her gaze.

PLATE VIII

WILLOW

COMMON NAME: Willow, the Silver Leaf Fairy

OTHER NAME: Fairy of the Silent Forest

SIGHTING DATE: February 15, 1999, 9:30 a.m.

SIGHTING LOCATION: Albany, Georgia

PEAK SIGHTING SEASON: Mid February[5]

HISTORY: Willow is regarded as a classic tree fairy. Earliest recorded sightings date back to A.D. 800. Florida Seminoles call her Tree Shadow, and associate her with mangroves and willow trees. Farther north, the Cherokee call her Silver Ghost, as she is usually seen among silver birch trees.

LURE: Bound sage on a bed of silver birch bark set in the shadow of the tallest tree

NOTES: Willow appeared, moving quickly from tree to tree, and I could only see her when she was in motion. When she was still, she blended with the trees. I ended up taking two rolls of film, just shooting in her general direction. I didn't get a good look at her until I got the film back.

5. *Willow's sighting season is only ten days long (reason is unknown), and she is said to roam from Florida to North Carolina, so I was extremely lucky to catch a glimpse of her.*

PLATE IX

NIMM

COMMON NAME: Nimm, the Purple-Blue Witch Fairy

OTHER NAME: Bitter Tear Fairy

SIGHTING DATE: March 10, 1999, from midnight to dawn

SIGHTING LOCATION: The Neolithic goddess temples of Malta

PEAK SIGHTING SEASON: Around spring equinox[6]

HISTORY: Records of Nimm date back to the Sumerian civilization over 5,000 years ago, when it was believed that gods and goddesses ruled the earth. She was said to be a creature of intoxicating beauty, desired by gods and men alike—though she rejected them all. Over time, she grew so obsessed with the imperfections of living things she vowed to punish all who crossed her path. According to legend those who dare never return.

LURE: Love poems of Pablo Neruda

NOTES: I wandered through the ruins late into the night, reciting poetry. At one point, I stopped before a shattered temple, lost in a soulful phrase. When I looked up, Nimm looked back at me! I stared at her, heard the shutter click with infinite slowness before the camera fell from my hand. Against my will, I took a step toward her and she smiled. Her eyes mesmerized me, and as I looked into them the world grew silent and still. After what seemed like only a minute, hours had passed and it was morning. I would have stood there forever had not a creature clad in yellow passed between Nimm and me, breaking my gaze. I snatched up my camera and got off a couple of shots,[7] and when I turned back, Nimm was gone. Empty and exhausted, I lay down and fell into a dreamless sleep that lasted twenty hours.

6. *Nimm is a fairy of the night, and Maltese legend has it that she often appears around the spring equinox, when the balance shifts and day becomes longer than night.*

7. *PLATE X, Unknown Fairy, following page.*

PLATE XI

MORAI

COMMON NAME: Morai, the Sea-Green Fairy
OTHER NAME: Spirit of the Loch
SIGHTING DATE: March 31, 1999, 8:40 a.m.
SIGHTING LOCATION: Loch Lomond, Scotland
PEAK SIGHTING SEASON: After the last frost[8]
HISTORY: According to legend, a small band of Sea-Green Fairies, originally from the bogs of Holland, migrated to the Scottish lochs in the seventeenth century to escape Amsterdam's growing population. Feeling that they were driven from their home, they bear a longstanding grudge against humans. Morai and her companions are treated with caution by locals, a number of whom claim to have been pulled underwater while fishing or swimming.
LURE: Narcissus and daffodils along the water's edge
NOTES: Morai appeared before I was prepared. I'd swum out to the mouth of a small cove to look across the loch. When I turned to swim back, Morai rose from near the water's edge. My initial surprise gave way to alarm as she drew closer. As I began to panic, she moved faster. I just barely made it ashore. I turned to her, heart pounding, and took my photos.

8. *Morai has never adjusted to Scotland's bitter winters. Sightings abound as winter gives way to spring, and Morai comes out of hiding.*

PLATE XII

LAUREL

COMMON NAME: Laurel, the Purple Sleeping Fairy
OTHER NAME: Talisman of the Unprotected
SIGHTING DATE: April 17, 1999, 7:00 p.m.
SIGHTING LOCATION: Ainaloa, Hawaii
PEAK SIGHTING SEASON: March–April; early spring
HISTORY: I read in the manuscript that this fairy appears as a small child locked in eternal sleep. According to local lore, her unguarded sleep embodies the essence of vulnerability. She lies unprotected yet sleeps unafraid, a symbol of power to the most helpless of creatures. She sleeps surrounded by colorful beads of light.[9]
LURE: I did not need a lure for Laurel, since the glow of light surrounding her revealed her location.
NOTES: I first spotted the colored lights as I skirted a waterfall at the edge of the forest. I climbed a tree and saw that, as I had hoped, they were circling the sleeping Laurel. I took some photos, then climbed down next to her. I was close enough to touch her, and I realized with a shock that there was nothing to prevent me from doing so. I reached out my hand, but at the last instant something made me stop. As I climbed up for one more photo, Laurel turned over in her sleep. I left as quietly as possible.

9. *Some say the beads of light are the colorful auras of fire fairies, while others claim they are an extension of Laurel herself. Either way, they add to her vulnerability by making her easy to discover for those in search of her.*

PLATE XIII

AUGUSTINE

COMMON NAME: Augustine, the Violet Bride Fairy

OTHER NAME: Fairy of the Tender Heart

SIGHTING DATE: April 28, 1999, dusk

SIGHTING LOCATION: Outside a mansion near the Seine, Paris

PEAK SIGHTING SEASON: Late April–May; flowers in bloom

HISTORY: Augustine was originally a member of a family of royal fairies whose mission it was to maintain the balance between nature and humanity. To that end, they eavesdropped on kings and queens, priests, artists, and revolutionaries, and sometimes appeared in dreams or disguises to influence important decisions. In her role as a matchmaker, Augustine fostered countless romances across Europe, until one day in a lilac garden she had a vision of her counterpart, her soulmate, and chose to pass a portion of eternity in a vigil of hope for the arrival of her love.

LURE: Bouquet of lilacs[10]

NOTES: I was walking along a stone wall when a hand reached out from it and grabbed the bouquet. It was Augustine. To my surprise, seeing her locked into the wall was not the sad experience I expected it to be. Rather, it filled me with hope and a buoyant optimism that lingered for weeks.

---

10. *Lilac season was still a few weeks away, making the lure all the more appealing to Augustine.*

PLATE XIV

D I A

COMMON NAME: Dia, the Fuchsia Moss Fairy
OTHER NAME: Fairy of Harmony and Light
SIGHTING DATE: May 11, 1999, 1:00 p.m.
SIGHTING LOCATION: Portofino, Italy
PEAK SIGHTING SEASON: May–June; spring
HISTORY: This lighthearted, energetic fairy has been spotted around creeks and streams playing in the tall grass at the water's edge. The majority of her sightings are in the forests of Eastern Europe, so I was surprised to find her along the Italian Riviera.[11] I was actually searching for the Pale-Green Fern Fairy, whom I never found.
LURE: Pink snapdragons and pansies
NOTES: Though she kept her distance, she was the only fairy who spoke to me. She said: "The fragrance of flowers, the play of shadows and light, the gleam on the grass—these are the keys to your innocence." And as she spoke, a patch of grass shimmering in the sun reminded me of my childhood, and I was filled with a distant but familiar sense of peace.

---

11. *There is some evidence that Dia is a migratory fairy. She has been sighted as far away as Corsica.*

PLATE XV

OPHELIA

COMMON NAME: Ophelia, the Pearl-White Fairy

OTHER NAME: South Seas Fairy

SIGHTING DATE: June 21, 1999, 3:20 p.m.

SIGHTING LOCATION: In the Bismarck Sea near Madang, Papua New Guinea

PEAK SIGHTING SEASON: Late June–July, The Calms[12]

HISTORY: Ophelia lives in the sea off the coast of New Guinea, where she can be seen exploring the turquoise waters. Locals claim that she is seeking clues to the nature of her soul. She began her search thousands of years ago and has not stopped, even for a moment.

LURE: Black volcanic sand in an abalone shell, placed outside a sea cave

NOTES: I spent several days diving through the waters around Ophelia's favorite spots, waiting for her to show herself. I thought I saw her once or twice in the distance, scouring the coral beds for obscure signs of her true identity, but each time she moved on before I could reach her. On about the fourth day, as I dove down, Ophelia rose from the depths and swam straight for me. She circled me several times, just inches away, studying me carefully. In her hand she held the abalone shell, which she handed back to me with a wistful shake of her head. Then she slowly swam away in ever widening circles.

12. *The Calms is a seasonal weather pattern that covers the South Pacific, making the water tranquil and visibility nearly unlimited.*

PLATE XVI

CEDAHLIA

COMMON NAME: Cedahlia, the Golden Angel Fairy

OTHER NAMES: Guardian of the Pure Heart, Fairy of the Celestial Kingdom

SIGHTING DATE: June 28, 1999, 5:35 p.m.

SIGHTING LOCATION: Urubamba Valley, Peru

PEAK SIGHTING SEASON: Unknown

HISTORY: From the lush Peruvian highlands to the Bolivian High Plateau, there exist local legends about Cedahlia, believed to be the purveyor of peace and compassion.

LURE: Conflict

NOTES: Though it was time to return home with my findings, stepping back into my old life promised to be an unsettling experience. I desperately wanted to continue my quest. As luck would have it, as I was preparing to leave Papua New Guinea, I crossed paths with a Bolivian Kallawaya[13] (Medicine Man), and he told me about Cedahlia, a fairy not mentioned in the original manuscript. Though my heart leapt at one more chance to see a fairy, the delay of my return home only heightened my anxiety.

This was my state of mind as I flew to Peru and hiked across a valley high in the Andes. A couple of hours into the hike, as I was resting, a quick movement caught my eye. I turned and saw Cedahlia crouching in a clearing a few yards away. As she watched me, I felt something stir within me and my fears inexplicably began to dissipate. As they vanished, a rainbow formed behind Cedahlia and I somehow knew that my journey had only just begun. I tossed my camera in my pack and headed home—to show the world what I had seen.

13. *My encounter with the Kallawaya was suspiciously providential, but it wasn't until later that I realized how odd it was to find a Medicine Man from the High Andes in the South Pacific.*

his book contains the results of my quest, the first set of fairy photographs the world has ever seen. And though they closely mirror what I saw with my own eyes, nothing can compare to the experience of watching a fairy rising from a lake, vanishing into the roots of a tree, peering through a glacier wall.

For future explorers, I have documented my expedition and what I learned along the way, and I believe my techniques will prove invaluable. It was an unprecedented journey, and it took me far beyond the boundaries of what I once considered the world of science. It was also a personal journey, as what I encountered forced me to open my mind and reevaluate my understanding of reality. The world will never look the same.

I have always been a practical person, a woman of science. My job is to follow the trail of evidence, wherever it leads, and arrange it in a way that sheds light on the mysteries of life. As an archeologist, I am accustomed to sifting through the strata, and I feel that what I have uncovered here is a small cross section of an uncharted realm. If there is one thing I have learned in the last year, it is that despite centuries of rigorous study, the unknown far outweighs the known.

Never would I have discovered the world of fairies on my own, and it was more than blind luck that led me to them. I now believe that it was the Unknown Fairy (see Plates V, X) who delivered the original unfinished manuscript to me and set me on this path. Though I was unable to get a well-defined photograph of her, out of all the fairies she remains the most vivid in my memory. She most certainly rescued me from disaster more than once.

I wonder how it could be that I never saw these amazing creatures before. And considering that they can be found throughout the world, why haven't more people seen them? I hope that my next expedition will shed some light on this mystery. For now, all I know is they are out there. They exist. This book is my living proof.

Suza Scalora

New York City, 1999

To Joanna Cotler and Mary Mandis for believing

Photography & art direction: Suza Scalora

Story: Suza Scalora & Darius Helm

Makeup: Susan McCarthy for Shu Uemura & Robin Schoen

Hair: Gerald DeCock, Stacey Ross, Jeff Francis & Dennis Lanni

Digital imaging: Suza Scalora & Jayme Thornton

Styling: Micaela Toledo

Set design: Remco Van Vliet for Van Vliet & Trap,

John Robinson & Todd Kenworth

Fairy dressings exclusively by Elisa Jimenez for The Hunger World

Wings: Zoe Joeright, Penelope Pattee, Laurentino Azevedo,

Mari O'Connor, Elisa Jimenez, Barrett Motroni, Rohan Sen,

Manolo, Joseph & Donna McElroy

Wing ice sculpture designed by: artist Joe O'Donoghue

of Ice Fantasies Inc. Brooklyn, NY

Jewelry: Erickson Beamon, Manolo & D'Drennan

Hairpieces: Colette Malouf

The Fairies: Angie Grgat, Satia Arteau, Dana Douglas, Manon

Van Gerkan, Raquel Azevedo, Marieme Dijo, Michaella Warren,

Harley Kinberg, Amy Nemec, Chandra North, Guenevere

Rodriguez, Benji Baker, Michelle Rozmarin, Sophie Peebles

Book design: Alicia Mikles

Production manager: Ruiko Tokunaga

Background paintings: Suza Scalora

The Fairies Copyright © 1999 by Suza Scalora Printed in Singapore. All rights reserved
http://www.harpercollins.com Library of Congress Cataloging-in-Publication Data Scalora, Suza.
The fairies : photographic evidence of the existence of another world / by Suza Scalora
p.   cm.   "Joanna Cotler Books"   Summary: After mysteriously receiving a copy of an old
manuscript, an archaeologist sets off around the world to photograph and document the existence
of a variety of fairies.   ISBN 0-06-028234-7   1. Fairies—Fiction. I. Title. PZ7.S27915Fai
1999 98-52052 [Fic]—dc21 CIP AC 1 2 3 4 5 6 7 8 9 10 ❖ First Edition